HAPPY BIRTHDAY AND LOVE TO SASHA FROM GRANNY AND GRAMPA

The Magic Paintbrush

by

ROBIN MULLER

Viking Kestrel

VIKING KESTREL

Published by the Penguin Group

Viking Penguin, a division of Penguin Books USA Inc.,

40 West 23rd Street, New York, New York 10010, U.S.A.

Penguin Books Ltd, 27 Wrights Lane, London W8 5TZ, England

Penguin Books Australia Ltd, Ringwood, Victoria, Australia

Penguin Books Canada Ltd, 2801 John Street, Markham, Ontario, Canada L3R 1B4

Penguin Books (N.Z.) Ltd, 182–190 Wairau Road, Auckland 10, New Zealand

Penguin Books Ltd, Registered Offices: Harmondsworth, Middlesex, England

First published in Canada by Doubleday Canada Limited, 1989

First American edition published 1990

10   9   8   7   6   5   4   3   2   1

ISBN: 0-670-83167-0

Design: The Dragon's Eye Press

Typeset in 11½ pt Berthold Joanna by Trigraph Inc.

Printed and bound in Hong Kong by Everbest Inc.

*To Sara and Melanie Irvine
and
to my brother Lawrence, who
gave me my first paintbrush.*

ONG AGO there lived an orphan boy called Nib. He couldn't read, he couldn't write, he couldn't even tell you how old he was. But he did know how to draw, and that was good, because more than anything else in the world, he wanted to be an artist.

Nib was so poor that he couldn't afford pens or brushes or paints. Instead, he followed the charcoal burner's cart that rumbled and bounced through the cobbled streets, and picked up the little black sticks that fell out.

With these charcoal sticks, Nib sketched on scraps of crates and boxes that piled up behind the market. Once he found a broken pencil in the gutter. When he sharpened it, it smelled of cedar, and the hard black lead tasted cold and sweet. On the back of a poster that had blown from a wall Nib drew a picture of a seagull, carefully shading in every feather and claw, finishing with its bright, mischievous eye.

He gazed with delight at his work. "One day," Nib cried, "I will make pictures so real that people will think they are alive."

During the day Nib did odd jobs to pay for the bowl of thin soup that kept him alive, but in the evening he hung around the outdoor cafés, listening to the artists arguing with each other over endless glasses of wine. When the final bottle was drained, the last candle flame snuffed and the streets were wrapped in a velvet shadow, Nib made his way home to the bridge by the river.

One night, as he picked his way through the gloom, he was startled by a terrible cry, then another, followed by the heavy thuds of a cudgel. The cry came again, more desperate and painful, followed by more blows and muffled curses.

Nib was terrified, and shrank deeper into the shadow, but something about the helplessness and pain in the cry for help pierced his heart. Without thinking, Nib darted toward the sound, knocking over a bucket in his haste. It boomed in the darkness. Seizing a stick, Nib thumped the bucket and shouted at the top of his lungs: "C'mon, lads, let's get 'em!" He raced forward as though he had a gang of river rats at his heels, eager to pound the living daylights out of anyone foolish enough to get in their way.

Ahead of him Nib could hear the clash of hobnail boots fleeing down the alley. Crumpled against the wall he found a very old man, his face waxen in the dim light. "Thank you," the man gasped. "Those men, they would have killed me."

"It's all right," said Nib. "You're safe now."

At his refuge under the bridge Nib gently tended the old man. The other poor waifs who sheltered there offered their tattered rags to bandage his cuts, and Sara the watercress girl, who had saved one small bunch for her supper, gave it to the old man so he would have something fresh to eat. Warmed by the children's kindness, he went to sleep.

The next day Nib helped the old man back to his home, a lonely garret at the top of a rickety stair. Nib lit a candle and peered around. Books and scrolls filled the cupboards and shelves; cloths embroidered with strange letters hung from the ceiling, and the working table was covered with pens and pots of coloured ink.

Nib puzzled over the writing and the intricate decorations. "Are you an artist?" he asked shyly. His question was greeted with a laugh.

"In a way, yes. But not in the way you mean. I inscribe words—secret words—and make them beautiful. But pictures of this world I do not make."

"I want to be an artist," said Nib fervently. "I want to paint pictures so real that people will think they are alive!"

The old man looked at Nib thoughtfully. "Do you?" he said. "Then I shall help you." He shuffled among his boxes and chests and then pulled open a small drawer. "Ah, here it is!"

He held up an intricately carved wooden box and pressed a small clasp. The lid popped open to reveal a palette, rows of paint tablets and one beautiful red paintbrush with golden hairs.

"This, my little friend, is for you." He held out the box. "The brush has been used to adorn the Words of Life, and the power of life is in its touch. It will help you make pictures while you see with your eyes. But one day you will learn to see with your heart, and then you will no longer have need of it."

Nib was speechless with wonder. "Take it, take it!" insisted the old man. "It is small return for your kindness." Nib accepted the box and stuttered his thanks, almost fearing the old man would change his mind.

"Don't thank me, little one! Just remember that our lives, this world and everything in it is the gift. Let your pictures be the thanks."

As Nib hurried down the street, he had the odd sensation that the world was changing around him. He glanced back to the old man's garret, but it was gone. A stone wall stood where moments before he had descended a stair.

"I must be dreaming," he said, and clutched the box ever more tightly. At least that was real. He hurried back to his home under the bridge.

Nib smoothed out his picture of the seagull and opened the paint box. "Now I can finish you." Carefully he brushed in the colours. They seemed to flow and shade by themselves. The bird was beginning to look real. Soon everything was complete except for the little spot of brightness on the eye. Holding his breath and biting his lip, Nib touched a tiny dab of white on the spot. "There..." he murmured.

With a squawk and a terrific flurry of wings, the gull burst off the page—bowling Nib over in its flight. The sheet before him was empty. High above the bird circled, flying freely in the grey sky.

Sara, the watercress girl, heard the commotion and ran over. She gazed at the blank paper. "Nib," she said, "what happened to your picture of the seagull?"

Nib smiled and looked in wonder at the paintbrush.

The next day in the market square, Nib settled down beside a flower stall. With his paint box beside him and a board balanced on his knees, he gazed at a freshly blooming rose. The petals curled open with a crimson blush and drops of dew clung to the stem.

Nib touched his brush to the colours and then to the board. As he worked, the rose seemed to rise from the surface of the wood. Finally Nib dotted in the spots of light on the dew drops—and the flower tumbled to the ground!

"That boy just made the picture of a flower come to life!" shouted a bystander. "Impossible!" shouted another. "Do it again!" yelled yet another.

Nib did. He made a cat come to life, a dove, two pigs, a dozen chickens and another rose. An excited crowd gathered around him. "Do it again! Do it again!"

Suddenly a hand grasped his shoulder. Nib tried to wriggle free but it was no use. The hand belonged to Zagal, Captain of the King's Guard.

"I've been watching you, my little man," he growled, "and I know someone who would like to see that little trick of yours. Pick up your things, you're coming with me!"

Nib was taken to a massive grey building, dragged down a long dark hall and thrust into an enormous room.

He had never imagined anything like it. The floor was marble; velvet curtains framed the windows; delicate vases stood on polished black cabinets, and the walls were hung with rows of magnificent paintings.

"What have you brought me, Zagal?" demanded an irritated voice. A tall, elegantly dressed man turned toward them. It was the King. "What is this street urchin doing here?" he asked coldly.

"Forgive me, Your Majesty, but this boy did the most amazing thing. I saw him painting a flower—and the very moment he finished it, it came to life." Zagal pulled the rose Nib had painted from his pocket. "Then he painted a cat, a dove, pigs, some chickens. And they all come to life!" Zagal waved to his attendants and the animals Nib had painted were herded into the room.

"You imbecile!" screamed the King as a terrified chicken landed on his head. "How dare you bring a barnyard into my chambers!"

"Give me but a moment, Your Majesty," pleaded Zagal, "and I will prove what I say is true."

Zagal thrust Nib down in front of a jade lion that stood on a nearby table. "Paint that, boy, or you will be sorry you were ever born!"

Nervously Nib studied the little statue. Then he opened his box and began to paint. "Not bad," muttered the King as the brush danced over the board. "The boy has talent."

"Wait!" whispered Zagal. "Just wait!" A few minutes later Nib brushed in the final details of the jade lion. The instant he did so, it tumbled from the board and onto his lap.

"Let me see that!" snapped the King. He held the jade lion up to the light, then stared at Nib. "Well, my little artist," he said, "isn't it lucky that fate has brought you to me? We will be friends, great friends."

"Yes, Your Majesty. That would be nice," said Nib. "But please may I go home now?"

The King looked at him in astonishment, and then he burst out laughing. "Go? You will never go! You are far too precious. You will stay here with me—making the things I crave."

"No!" cried Nib. "You already have everything anybody could want! You don't need my help. Let me go home!"

The King seized Nib by the collar. "You will do as I say," he hissed. "Zagal, take this guttersnipe to the dungeons and lock him up. A night spent in the company of rats may help him change his mind."

The dungeon was dark and cold, and rats scurried between Nib's feet, but he didn't mind. As soon as the guards were gone, Nib took out his brush. Colours swirled and danced as he painted a roaring fire, a comfortable chair, flowers to sweeten the air, and a table piled high with food. "Not bad," he sniffed, mimicking the King. "Not bad at all."

The next morning, after breakfast, the King announced, "That young rascal must be so terrified and hungry that he will agree to anything. I will pay him a visit so he can see how forgiving I can be."

The door to the dungeon was thrown open, but when the King looked in and saw how comfortable Nib had made it, he screamed with rage. "Guards, seize the prisoner, beat him, cage him, load him with chains!" But before they could lay hands on him, Nib was gone. He had painted a tunnel and escaped. The guards squeezed into the tunnel, but they became hopelessly stuck.

"Search the city!" bellowed the King. "Every gutter and attic. And don't stop till you find him!"

Nib was in great danger. Everywhere the King's guards were waiting to arrest him. Posters appeared throughout the kingdom offering huge rewards for the capture of the boy who could bring pictures to life.

Nib sat by the road and gazed sadly at his paint box. "Perhaps I should throw you away," he said. "I can never use you without being caught." But then he had an idea. "I will go on painting, but I won't finish my pictures. Then they won't come to life."

As a travelling artist Nib journeyed from town to town. He painted fantastic castles perched on the sides of mountains, and busy ports where tall ships arrived with exotic fruit, coloured birds and strange animals. Rich and famous people begged him to paint portraits of them, offering fortunes for his services. But with every picture Nib never forgot to leave out some little detail, so his secret would not be revealed.

Nib should have been happy, but he wasn't. He could paint beautiful scenes better than anyone, but the more he looked for beauty, the more he found pain and ugliness. He saw huge factories built in pleasant meadows, little country towns swallowed by cities and turned into slums, and gentle animals beaten and neglected by their owners.

Disheartened, Nib sat down by a brook which had been poisoned by a factory's waste. "The paintbrush is magic," he said to himself. "Maybe I can paint it better." Setting up his easel, he painted a clear babbling stream. But every stroke became muddy and black. "The brush will only let me paint what I see with my eyes," he sighed unhappily, "not what I see with my heart."

Lonely and sad, Nib returned to the city to find the friends he had lived with under the bridge. But when he arrived at his old home, no one was there.

He strolled over to the square where he had first painted the rose. He gazed fondly at the crowds and the buildings—and then caught sight of a familiar figure huddled in a doorway. It was Sara the watercress girl, but she was so different from when he had known her. Her face was thin and pinched, and a strange brightness was in her eyes.

"Sara, what has happened to you?" Nib cried.

"Oh, Nib!" the girl replied. "Palace guards came looking for you. They drove us out of our place under the bridge and burnt all our things. We had to sleep wherever we could— and I got sick. Help me, Nib, I'm so hungry and cold." She collapsed on the ground coughing.

"Sara, Sara, I'm sorry," cried Nib. Quickly he opened his box and painted a beautiful woollen shawl and tucked it around her shoulders. Then he painted a bowl full of oranges, pears and grapes. But Sara was too weak to eat.

"I will paint you well!" he said desperately. "It will work— it *must* work." And he began to paint the girl's portrait, not as she was, but healthy and happy, with clear eyes and rosy cheeks.

It was no use. With every stroke the colours darkened and cracked. "It's all my fault," he cried pitifully. "I wish I had never taken the old man's gift." Tears ran down his cheeks and splashed onto the picture. As they did so, something wondrous began to happen. The colours suddenly brightened, filling the portrait with light, and when Nib looked up, Sara was standing before him, smiling.

"You're well again!" he cried joyously. "Everything is going to be all right!"

"It certainly is!" a wicked voice bellowed behind him. Nib was yanked to his feet and twisted around. He found himself looking into the cruel eyes of Zagal. "I knew that one day you would return to your little friend here. All I had to do was keep watch. Now you're both coming with me!"

At the palace the King was delighted to see Nib. "So, my little artist," he crowed, "you tried to escape me. How foolish of you! It won't happen again, I assure you."

The King smiled and rubbed his hands together. "I have some work for you to do. And if you refuse, you will force me to be nasty to your little friend here." He waved at Sara. "Very, very nasty."

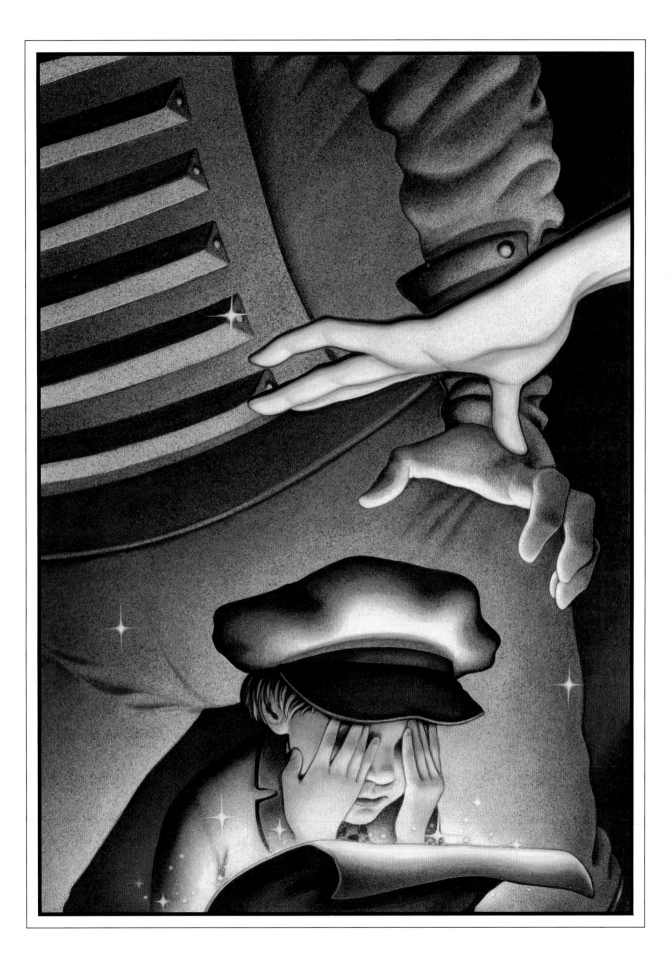

Day after day, Nib sat in the gallery, painting pearls, sapphires, gold doubloons, bars of silver. The King never tired of watching him, and took a childish pleasure in counting the treasure as it fell from Nib's board. "Soon I will be rich enough to pay for anything I want—even the biggest army in the world," he gloated.

Nib was terrified at the thought, but the King's boast gave him an idea. "Your Majesty," he began, "Instead of painting gold and jewels, why don't I just paint what you want and you shall have it?"

"But what if it's something really big, like a fleet of warships?"

"I can paint that!" said Nib eagerly. "I can paint big things on the wall, and you can just walk into the picture. I'll show you."

Standing on a chair, Nib started to paint. The brush flew in his hand as he went: oak hulls, tall masts, brass fittings, rows of shining cannons. Soon a fleet of magnificent warships seemed to be moored only a short distance away. Finally Nib painted a gangplank leading right onto the deck of the nearest ship.

"The royal navy, Your Majesty. Please step aboard."

The King looked warily at the picture. Everything looked normal. Sailors were coiling ropes and the vessels were gently rising on the tide.

"Very well, I shall." He ordered Zagal and all his men to follow him on board. From the deck he called out, "This is marvellous. With these ships I can conquer the world. Paint me a breeze so we can set sail."

Nib painted the sails beginning to fill with wind. "More, more!" shouted the King. Nib worked furiously. Soon the peaceful sea started to dance as he painted wave after wave. Still the King yelled for more. Under Nib's brush the clear blue sky turned grey, fluffy white clouds turned black, and foam leapt from the crest of the waves.

"Enough!" screamed the King, but Nib's brush still flew. The sun disappeared behind a cloud and thunder shook the sky. The King's cries were almost drowned as the fleet began to be swept out to sea. "Enough! Stop this at once!"

"All right," yelled Nib over the din of the storm, "I *will* stop! I don't need this brush to paint my pictures." And, seizing his paint box and brush, he hurled them into the raging water.

"Scoundrel!" screamed the King. Suddenly there was a blinding flash of lightning and a terrible crash. The King, the fleet and the sea were gone. Nib was staring at a blank wall.

Without the King, life in the country improved. Soon the meadows were filled with wild flowers, and the rivers ran fresh and sweet. One day, Nib and Sara were happily strolling through the city when something caught Nib's eye. He stooped to pick up a little black stick from between the cobbles. He rolled it gently in his fingers, and on a piece of paper sketched Sara's portrait. "The best pictures," he laughed as he looked at her smiling face, "are the ones you make with your heart."